Honey Money Moon
Tryst with lust

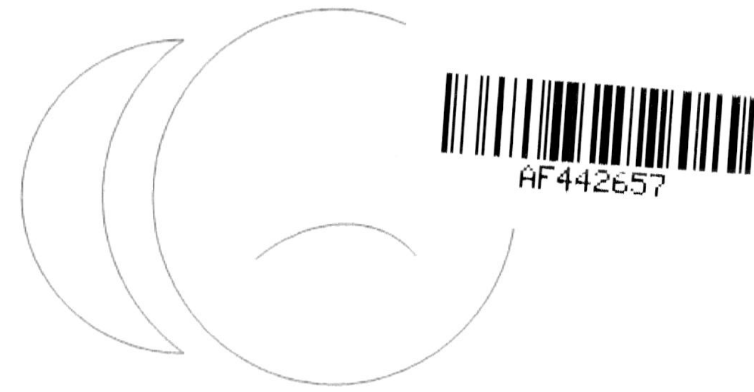

SATISH BATAKALA

ACKNOWLEDGEMENTS

This is my second book published after a gap of eight years.

To my wife, for challenging my stubbornness and keeping my ego in check.

To my daughter, for making me fall in love once again with her cute innocence.

ABOUT THE AUTHOR

I was born in Vishakhapatnam, India in 1985. I did my MBA from IIM Calcutta and B. TECH from IIIT Hyderabad. I don't promote porn, prostitution or sexual exploitation of any gender of any sort. I am passionate about space exploration and hope that we are able to realize interstellar travel within my lifetime. The story, all names, characters and incidents portrayed are fictitious. No identification with actual persons, places or buildings is intended or should be inferred.

Happy reading!

Contents

PROLOGUE

Toddler: "Papa…Moon…Moon"

Dad: "Wait. Have patience, my cutie pie"

Toddler: "I want to see bunny, the bunny on the moon"

Dad: "My sugar plum, you see all these tall towers of buildings. They are blocking our view of the Moon. We need to walk for another ten minutes out of this concrete jungle to get a clear view of the night sky "

The toddler noticed an old humongous communication tower right in the middle of the road. Her favorite role in her imaginative play was that of an astronaut and she likened the tower to a rocket.

Toddler: "My teacher told me that humans visited Moon in the past. Let's go in a rocket to visit the moon."

"3-2-1 and blast off!"

Dad: "And you blindly believed her? Kids need to be more curious and should pester teachers with many questions. And that is the reason I enrolled you into a Montessori school."

It is ironical that as we become adults, we are forced to accept things and not ask questions - curiosity killed the cat, after all.

The color of the sky was a tad bluish and the toddler could see the dark outline of bats fly in the moonlight.

Toddler: "Papa, but isn't it full moon tonight? I am really scared"

Dad: "Why fear when I am here? Papa will protect you from any monsters as long as he is alive"

He was Mufasa for his three-year-old little cub. As a single dad, he donned the dual role of father and mother and put his best foot forward to ensure that his cub always roared in delight. He was also a real estate mogul, owning luxury properties all over the world.

He was acting loony now by flexing his non-existent biceps. At the bend of the road, they spotted his daughter's regular hangout, an ice cream truck owned by an immigrant in a foreign land. He shared a good rapport with the duo.

Ice cream vendor: "Baby, don't you want a yummy yummy ice cream tonight?"

Furious dad to vendor: "Oh no, not you again. You have spoilt my daughter as she can't sleep unless I buy her an ice cream every night"

Ice cream vendor: "Everyone here knows that your daughter is obsessed with peeking at the Moon. And to top it all off, you have named her after the Moon"

Dad was silenced by the perfect riposte.

All of them were staring at the luminous Moon. The toddler was taken aback as she was unable to find the moon rabbit tonight. There was eerie silence for a minute or two, similar to the silence of the enigmatic universe.

It was broken by a high-pitched snapping sound, followed by a thud.

Toddler screamed "Papa...Papa…wake up. I got a boo boo" as she was covered in a splatter of red blood.

A group of ten employees dressed in suits are shitting their pants as they are prepping for the big pitch to their fearless CEO. Everywhere else, fun and frolic marked Lunar New Year celebration. No siree, not at Venuxx Corporation. No, it is not a porn company. However, it does explore other kind of bodies.

Last year, the best pitch was about extracting precious Gold from the Core of Earth. A meteor containing elements and a metal unknown to mankind crashed into the Pacific Ocean last year. After retrieving meteor contents from abysmal depths, it was discovered that this new metal could drill into anything and could withstand the heat of the Sun.

The winning pitch of year 2028 was on generating energy more efficient than power of the stars. Under controlled conditions, when an object is dropped from a particular altitude in the sky, Earth's gravitational energy is converted to immense kinetic energy if object is able to achieve near speed of light. And upon touchdown of the object on Earth, the boundless potential energy created is tapped to light up and power the entire world.

Venuxx was rated #1 in Fortune 500 list over the past three years. Venuxx has three primary business lines: Space, Core Earth and Ocean Floor exploration. They spun off from their parent company, a top global real estate firm, ten years ago. XX in the company name alludes to two X chromosomes. All of their employees identified themselves as Asexual, though they were born as girls biologically.

Few centuries ago, when humans followed societal gender binary - male and female, it was pretty straightforward to figure out sex of any human. In the current age, in all of identity cards of a person, sex information has been replaced by gender identity and there are more than fifteen gender identities as to how people describe, present, and feel about themselves. The governments have reservation in the name of gender identities and a few dishonest people fake their gender identity to easily get jobs, in an otherwise competitive market.

Yue, CEO of Venuxx, is the Queen Bee. She by nature is the polar opposite of Aphrodite, ancient Greek goddess of love and beauty. She is a gorgeous woman in her early forties and is averse to dating. While many men are attracted by her looks, they never could muster enough confidence to speak to her à la Raj's character in the popular series Big Bang Theory. The word on the street is that even if there were a hypersexual guy daring enough to flirt with her, she would invite him for a cup of coffee in a secret crypt and that the guy would never be seen again.

The main competitor of Venuxx in terms of market share and revenue is Marxy Private Limited. It is a wellness company and is led by its CEO, Madan. The company logo is an upside-down pineapple, which one often associates with symbol on doors of clandestine hotel rooms. Madan is a well-built man in his mid-30s and is the proverbial Sigma Male. Many a man was jealous of him because of his success with women. He was married previously, is father of a girl child and was surprisingly divorced by his wife last year.

Rumors were rife on social media that Yue and Madan dated in the past. No one knew if there was any truth in the news. But it made good headlines such as *"King Kong vs Godzilla"*, *"Sigma Male vs Alpha Female"*, *" The sting of the Queen Bee"* etc.

Alpha, Beta, and Omega personality types are believed to be borrowed from older behavior research on captive wolves. Alpha is leader of a pack and responsible for breeding to produce healthy offspring, Beta is second in hierarchy and is cooperative and naïve and Omega is dependent and submissive. Sigma is similar to Alpha type but with go-it-alone attitude and has nothing to do with the pecking order.

All types of wolf's howl at night. There is also a popular myth that humans turn into werewolves during Full Moon and could be killed only by a silver bullet. However, it is scientifically proven that howling of wolves has no connection with the Moon and their behavior might just be a social rally.

MOON IS THE CYNOSURE OF ALL EYES

Since the beginning of mankind, it was the rich and powerful who took decisions on the behalf of people on Earth. Common people had no say in it. Humans waged many wars and the sections that suffered the most were the soldiers and civilians. Losing side generally must cede something to the winner, be it money, territory, or sovereignty. In addition, their women were raped and children tortured or trafficked.

As long as homo sapiens are alive, there will be wars to satiate their lust for territory or resources. If it were left to a responsible Artificial Intelligence to decide fate of life on Earth, humans would always be convicted in its court.

Animals also fight such territorial wars and are cruel towards the vanquished. However, it is the rational thinking ability of human mind that makes it tough for any other creature to challenge their dominance. Man-animal conflicts have been trending on social media.

Governments protect forests and buffer zones but the lust for real estate and resources leads to encroachment of these protected corridors, which are becoming smaller and smaller day by day. In rare scenarios, humans are attacked in these zones and animals are declared either as man-eating or as a pest and humans put a price on their heads.

At the end of second world war, the superpowers

understood the devastation of wars and signed nuclear treaties to maintain peace. United Nations was created to stop wars between countries. The problem with peace is that it isn't good for business. And powerful businesses call the shots on behalf of governments. Hence, even in today's modern world, we still see countries waging wars and everyone else being a mute spectator.

In such a scenario, how do superpowers assert their dominance and control rest of the world? They looked towards the stars and that's how the political space race began. The United States of America, known for its pioneering technology, individualism and prodigious talent base due to influx of smart immigrants, emerged as a winner.

In the year 1969, humans landed on the Moon for the first time as part of Apollo program. It is celebrated across the world as One Giant Leap for Mankind. Manned moon landings stopped after 1972. USA blamed it on the humongous budget required to fund Apollo programs. It has been more than fifty years since a human set foot on the Moon.

Yue's secretary Chloe informed Yue that she has an important meeting the next day. All the corporate, political and uber rich bigwigs are on the invitee list of Luna Accords appointment. Yue loved the latest pitch related to mining on the dark side of the Moon made by her A team and wanted to get required approval to kick off the project.

On the next day, Yue stole the limelight at the Luna

Accords meeting with her presentation. All men and women were hypnotized by her intellect and beauty. During their conversations with the Alpha Female, Yue, they stuttered and shrugged their shoulders.

An eccentric billionaire, high on cocaine and who loved acting the cock of the walk, strutted towards Yue in a happy mood.

"I have a better plan for my woman of astonishing beauty. Let's nuke the poles of the Moon" he said sweating profusely.

In Indian mythology, Draupadi was objectified as her husband wagered on her in a game of dice. Despite her piteous pleas for help, all the onlookers, including her five noble husbands, turned a deaf ear as Dushasana dragged her by her hair while she was menstruating and started disrobing her. The Vastraharan was aborted midway due to the magical intervention of Lord Krishna. Now imagine the Moon in Draupadi's shoes. Will someone conjure up a robe to protect her modesty?

Yue smirked and asked Chloe to fix a personal appointment with him. He was encouraged by this and he placed his hand flirtatiously on Yue's bum. All of a sudden, an energetic young man approached Yue and pecked her on the cheek. The man was none other than Madan. The other male left the scene and started planning his date with Yue.

"You have an interesting idea. It is a big step in the

exploration of the universe and can contribute significantly towards development of humans as a race" Madan complimented Yue.

"Thank You. Do I know you?" asked Yue while pretending to wipe his kiss.

"I am Madan, CEO of Marxy. My presentation is up next." replied Madan

Yue felt that Madan was just another guy trying to use pick up lines and get into her impenetrable pants. But somehow, he seemed different as she could sense courage in his eyes. He had a silent allure that's irresistibly magnetic.

Madan threw a curveball at Yue by asking her "Have you thought about environmental impact to the Moon due to your mining project?"

"That is the reason we all have gathered here and are agreeing on the consequences. No one else has raised a voice against me" Yue replied.

"People who have gathered here represent only 1% of the population, that is the ultra-rich individuals. What about rest of the living beings who glance at the Moon during night? And what about the Moon? Did anyone take her consent?" retorted Madan.

The entire audience is looking at the couple in stunned silence and utter disbelief. Though Madan's firm was ranked second in the world, it didn't garner the same respect as Yue's firm. Madan was a lone wolf and a self-made man whereas Yue expanded her father's business into new frontiers.

A few minutes later, Madan took the spotlight and introduced himself. Before he could present his idea, he was taken aback by a question from the committee.

"So, Mr. Madan, everyone in the hall is telling us that you are the best guy in the world. They say that you have mastered the art of seduction. How do you attract the opposite sex with great panache?" enquired the committee.

"Respectful committee members, I would beg to differ regarding such rumors. I believe I am like a guy next door who follows the religion of love and speaks the language of truth. It would in our best interest to focus on the agenda" said Madan, trying his best not be trigged by such an insensitive remark.

After a few seconds, Madan gave his elevator pitch.

"The word honeymoon originated in medieval times from the practice of drinking Mead, a beverage made with honey, during the first month of the marriage. And this month is measured by one moon cycle. Now just imagine, if a partner is literally able to take his/her partner to the Moon on their honeymoon. And for this reason, I plan to setup an ecofriendly resort and spa on the Moon for couples to celebrate their coitus and immortalize their celestial love".

Yue yawned with disgust at his inane idea. She would never vote for any idea that was physical intimacy between humans.

Everyone in attendance sensed the heightened friction between Yue and Madan. They couldn't even fathom the impact on the world when the two most powerful human beings are at loggerheads with each other. The remaining pitches were blatantly disregarded. No decisions were taken on any lunar projects on that night.

Moon is the natural satellite of Earth and no one is sure of its origin. In 1957, Sputnik I was the first artificial satellite launched into space by the erstwhile Soviet Union. Since then, more than fifteen thousand satellites have been launched into space, out of which around eight thousand are still active in low-Earth orbit.

Many of the old satellites have fallen out of use. All of this space junk is orbiting Earth at speeds of up to 28,000 km/h and it poses an increasing risk of collision with any spaceship or rocket that is trying to escape Earth's gravitational pull. In a worst-case scenario, some of these defunct satellites might crash into Earth.

After reaching deadlock at the recent Luna Accords meeting, Madan became busy managing the space junk removal program. Marxy's pitch to remove space debris with the help of a few other countries was approved by the Luna Accords in their penultimate meeting. It was part of Marxy's corporate social responsibility initiatives.

In the meantime, Yue was gearing up to test the latest prototype of Venuxx's underwater suit. She took inspiration from the green exo-frame suit donned by the Max Ray character in the 1986 cartoon *Centurions*. It was designed similar to an automated *Iron Man* suit to move efficiently underwater and could easily obtain diving depth of 100 meters. And the best thing about the suit was that the person wearing it needn't know proper swimming.

"Are you out of your fucking mind? If you really want to die, there are hundreds of thousands of ways I can recommend you that lead to a better death" Chloe shouted at Yue.

Yue was at the edge of a boat in the middle of the warm Pacific Ocean and was ready to dive in alone with her suit, which was still untested in battle. Their boat was exactly above the deepest place on Earth, the Challenger Deep in the Mariana Trench. Chloe spotted another ordinary-looking boat approaching them. Madan and a few young European women were on the other boat. Their objective was to collect remains of a crashed satellite.

Unknown to Madan, a few influential people having stake in lunar projects crashed the satellite on purpose near Challenger Deep. A little birdie informed them that Yue would be testing her prototype suit in the same location and they wanted both of them to interact to bury the hatchet.

Chloe looked towards Madan for support to change Yue's mind. To her surprise, he couldn't care less and kept a calm demeanor. He made an intentional eye contact with Yue and then resumed his conversation with the European women, who were visibly entranced by Madan's physique. Madan was just in his boxer shorts and had a well-toned body while the two women giving him company were tall and thin, with well-proportioned bodies and striking features.

Yue took a plunge to try what no Man or Woman had ever achieved. Even though their boat had a couple more crew members, Chloe was bored to death and asked Madan if she could instead join them on their boat, to which he gladly agreed.

"You three seem to be having a lot of fun. Madan, I am pretty sure a stud like you can satisfy another young woman like me. The more the merrier" Chloe said flirtatiously.

Madan, who didn't believe in sweet talking, ignored her and honestly replied "Chloe, you are not the type of woman I prefer".

Chloe was taken aback. If you put Chloe in a room filled with hundred men, she could flirt with just about every man in the room and drive them crazy. She flirted with innocent men for fun and was never emotionally attached to those men. However, she was scared of Yue and never ever flirted with any man in front of her.

She quickly came to her senses and asked if the other two women were to his liking. To the dismay of the two young women, Madan gave an authentic response and said that they were just his friends helping him in the program.

"So, who is your type of woman? Does she exist in reality or is she fictional?" enquired Chloe.

"I value qualities like intelligence, maturity, loyalty, and respect in a woman" replied Madan.

"I am pretty sure you will stay single for the rest of your life. This is the curse of a young sexy woman. Or are you an aunty lover, that is a guy who prefers cougar?" joked Chloe.

Four hours passed by. After retrieving the fragments of the crashed satellite, Madan and the women in bikinis on board started dancing to some good music on the boat. Yue suddenly emerged out of water and climbed the boat. Her exo-frame suit was dripping wet and she carefully removed it to reveal herself in a scuba drysuit.

"Where the hell were you, Chloe? I was trying to communicate with you from the bottom of the Mariana Trench" Yue screamed at Chloe.

"I was trying to help these guys. I am pretty sure you remember Madan, the CEO of Marxy" said Chloe.

"Congratulations Yue!"

"Diving to the bottom of Mariana Trench is a landmark achievement in the history of mankind. Till today, we dived to such great depths using submersibles. Now, thanks to your exo-frame suit, ocean exploration will become much easier. You have made your parents proud" exclaimed Madan.

Chloe nudged Madan and whispered to him that Yue was an orphan. So much for creating a good impression. She also noticed that Madan was undressing Yue with his eyes and poked him gently. And the two European women in two-piece bikini were eyeing up Madan, which kind of made Yue jealous.

"Yue, don't move. There is a sn…sna…" Madan stammered while pointing towards Yue's boobs.

Madan spotted the tail of a banded sea snake sticking out of her dry suit. A single dose of its venom could kill ten fully grown men. Being a sigma male, Madan was not afraid of death. However, snakes were his worst nightmare and he was too stunned to speak.

Anyone who locked gaze with *Medusa* was turned into stone.

Yue immediately put her bare hands inside her dry suit, pulled out the venomous sea krait in a jiffy and casually threw it back into the ocean.

After a few hours, the sky turned dark and all the seven of them started playing a game of Mafia under the luminous Full Moon. In Mafia, there are 2 teams: the mafia and the villagers or townspeople. The mafia try to eliminate the villagers while the villagers try to guess who's in the mafia.

Mafia is played in night cycles and day cycles. In night cycles, mafia members "kill" villagers while everyone's eyes are closed. In day cycles, players accuse and eliminate people they think might be a part of the mafia. Accused players are allowed to give defenses and a vote takes place.

Madan noticed that Yue was an expert at this game. Whenever she was a mafia, she killed all the villagers and no one ever doubted her.

After having a blast playing the game, Chloe setup up candle light dinner for Madan and Yue. While Madan was waiting for food to arrive, Yue approached the dinner table wearing a stunning red tulle gown. Madan started fantasizing about their romance under the stars and the moonlit sky.

She blew away the candles and left after saying "Sorry to disappoint you darling. But I am not hungry tonight".

The Chinese zodiac, is a repeating 12-year cycle of animal signs and their ascribed attributes, based on the lunar calendar. In order, the zodiac animals are: Rat, Ox, Tiger, Rabbit, Dragon, Snake, Horse, Goat, Monkey, Rooster, Dog, Pig.

Yue was born with a silver spoon in the Year of the Snake. However, she was raised in a hidden village at the edge of a forest because of an unfortunate twist of fate. Her mom died during childbirth and her biological dad was killed by unknown assassin when she was still a toddler. She was raised by an ice cream vendor.

Given the circumstances of her father's death, the ice cream vendor strongly believed that there was an unknown threat to Yue's life and hid her from the outside world. Yue lovingly called him Appa and he tried to raise her as his own daughter. He was extremely hard-working by nature but somehow managed to eke out time to play with Yue.

Peek-a-boo! I see you.

He was playing with her a game of hide and seek. However, raising a toddler is no mean feat. Toddlers are like poop machines, throw tantrums and always say no.

No eat Appa! No sleep Appa! No school Appa!

At the behest of his fellow villagers, Appa unwittingly

married a woman known as Eramma in her early 20s to take good care of Yue. He made the ultimate sacrifice for his adopted daughter. He underwent vasectomy surgery to not have children of his own and hid this fact from his wife. Ironically, his wife was using inconceivable ways to conceive.

She would force herself on him every night and made love on a daily basis. Without his knowledge, she would mix Shilajit in his milk and made him eat drumstick vegetable curry every other day. Whenever Appa was in the house, she would dress scarcely and seduce him with her sexy gait. She would even stoop low to steal the umbilical cord from a woman who recently gave birth, dry it and consume it later in a hope to treat infertility.

A gullible Eramma also visited unregistered medical practitioners or quacks who operate in many tents by side of the road. Their banner claimed "Here is a cure for all diseases. We possess long years of traditional healing experience".

Quacks targeted people who did not feel too comfortable discussing the problems they are facing in the bedroom with doctors and took advantage of social reservations about discussing sexual problems. She didn't know that quacks usually provide steroids, which could lead to fungal infection. She fell for one of the guys operating a quack and started cheating on her husband. Appa couldn't catch them as quacks made it a point not to stay in one place for more than 10 to 15 days.

Eramma had exhausted all methods to get pregnant to no avail. The poor woman was mocked by villagers and was nicknamed barren woman. And she blamed Yue for everything and resented her.

Eleven years passed by. The celestial bodies in the night sky were playing a game of hide and seek with each other. The Moon, mostly embarrassed after being found, was rusty in color. Earth was blocking sunlight from reaching the Moon causing a total lunar eclipse. Entire village stayed at home after evening and avoided intake of food and water. Yue had sneaked out of home to peek at the Blood Moon. It was so strange being out there, knowing that there wasn't a living soul for miles around. She chanced upon a small white rock, which caught her attention. Yue picked up the rock, hid it in her dress and scurried home like a mouse.

On the very same night, Yue woke up with blood on her bed. She screamed her lungs out and called Appa for help. Appa requested his wife to handle the situation as the issue at hand seemed related to a woman's health. Eramma announced that Yue had her menarche and started yelling at Yue as she turned dirty, impure and unholy after her first menstruation. Owing to weird customs of the village, Yue was dressed in the same clothes for a week and not allowed to take bath. To celebrate this coming-of-age ceremony, Appa gifted her a new Langa Voni or a half saree. This marked her transition into womanhood.

It was a double body blow for Yue as her breasts started

developing one year ago. She trembled in fear as she walked on the streets. Many a time, she red-handedly caught the men in the village ogling at her chest. From a fifteen-year school going boy to a seventy-year-old man, every man she knew had only one job in hand, which was to gauge the size of her bosom and compare her two assets with various fruits. They placed bets to correctly guess the timeframe when the lemons would turn into melons.

The only man in the village she could trust was her Appa. He instilled in her the value of hard work and encouraged her to focus on her studies.

Eramma had a boring sex life. She had lost interest in her husband a few years into their marriage and was still childless. To beef up the image of herself, she blamed her husband for his lack of virility. Appa had a huge seven-inch dick when fully erect. Usually, women resort to blaming small penis size for lack of satisfaction during sex. Instead, she created a ruckus and falsely complained to him that because of his big size, she is experiencing a lot of pain in the vaginal area during mating.

This woman would never take the responsibility for her actions and always transferred the blame onto the scapegoat Appa for any situation. Appa could never vent the years of pent-up anger with his wife. In spite of finding his wife physically attractive, his angry mind forbade his body from being turned on and indulge in the act of love making.

Eramma helped Yue change her dirty cloth every month and slowly started noticing her beauty. There was no concept of sanitary pads in these remote villages. Slowly but surely, she became enamored of Yue. On one fateful night when her husband was away and Yue was fast asleep, she removed Yue's clothes and penetrated her pussy gently with her fingers. Then she used cucumbers to penetrate each other's vaginas and started licking Yue's tender nipples while pinching her own nipples. She continued this until she orgasmed and luckily Yue didn't wake up during the act.

The next morning, when Yue woke up, she realized that she had been wronged and started crying profusely. She had always pictured her first time with a charming prince. The cunning Eramma wanted to exploit Yue further, so she called the neighbors and blamed Appa for raping his adopted daughter. Before Appa could open his mouth, they started beating him with sticks for committing such a taboo act and handed him over to the local police station. Appa was imprisoned for five years. Yue was shattered and completely heartbroken.

"How could my loving Appa commit such a heinous crime?" a crestfallen Yue she said to herself.

A few months after this horrible incident, Eramma hatched a plot to curry favor with a grieving Yue by providing her tips on being a strong woman.

"A woman has untapped power from the time her periods start till her menopause. Think of this period as a boon rather than a bane. If a beautiful woman like you can leverage her body in a smart manner, she can bring the world to its feet" said Eramma to Yue.

"Oh god! Call me daddy! Fuck me hard"

Yue woke to loud noises emanating from Eramma's room. The door was purposefully left ajar. Yue saw that Eramma was on top of her naked boyfriend and was riding him as if he was an Arabian horse. Eramma noticed Yue from corner of her eye and whispered that she could join them and that they will train her to be good at sex.

Yue hated and rejected the bold proposal. Eramma then forced Yue to be a part of ménage à trois by resorting to blackmail by saying that she would stop Yue's schooling in case she refused again. Resigned to her fate, Yue had to relent to indulging in threesome. As she left the room tired and battered, she eavesdropped on the conversation of couple having an illicit affair.

"I am going to the city tomorrow to meet Yue's family lawyer. That stupid bitch doesn't realize that she is the daughter of one of the wealthiest men in the world, who died many years ago in a shootout. My husband and I took care of her ever since. She has not yet turned eighteen years and as her guardian, I can lay claim to her entire fortune" Eramma dropped a bombshell while confiding in her paramour.

Alas!

Eramma didn't wake up to see the light of day. She was swallowed and regurgitated by a giant 25-foot reticulated python which had sneaked into her room. Yue filled up her pockets with whatever coins she could find at home and boarded the city bus.

MADAN

There was a lot of commotion outside a five-year-old Madan's house. There were a few neighbor aunties and school teachers giggling, chattering and gossiping, with a tiny Madan in their midst. Madan's mom came out and was confused by the situation. The ladies asked her to bring his school bag to them. She obliged and went inside to fetch his bag. His mother knew Madan was naughty and was trying to guess what her son did this time around.

She opened the first zip of the unkempt bag in front of the women. There was a half empty water bottle made of plastic with some visible algae growth and the uneaten lunchbox. She had packed a healthy lunch box containing three Indian bread and Madan didn't eat a morsel of it. She made up her mind to take him to task once the crowd had dispersed.

The demoralized mother then opened the second zip of the school bag. Lo and behold, she was taken aback by contents inside it. She found bras of various colors and size. The ladies confessed that it was Madan who stole their innerwear from their balconies. They grinned cheekily and compared his misdeeds with the act of Lord Krishna stealing clothes of Gopikas on the banks of Yamuna River. According to them, this act of Madan was pardonable and very cute.

After they dispersed, Madan's mom was raging with anger.

In a fit of rage, she hit her son with a comb lying nearby and enquired as to why he did such an embarrassing act.

A crying Madan replied "Mom, I am not sure why I am curious or attracted to women's underwear"

This reply from her son left her speechless. She was wondering if it were genes of her estranged husband coming into play. Madan's father was a lothario and abandoned them for another young woman when Madan was just two years old. And Madan was breastfed until he turned four as his mother found it very hard to wean her baby from breastfeeding.

Years passed by. Madan was in his teens. His mother was a strict parent and left no stone unturned to ensure that he wasn't exposed to anything sexual. Madan was studying in an all-boys convent school and was allowed to use a mobile phone or tab only without internet. She tore away pages in magazines and newspapers having lingerie advertisements or any content she felt was explicit. He wasn't allowed to spend than more than five minutes in the bathroom or toilet. He could only play with his guy friends at his home and his friends never understood why he never visited their homes. He slept in the same double-bedded bedroom as his mother.

The setting of dense, moist and the largest tropical rainforest in the entire world was incredulously done. The theatre was filled with cacophony of too many animal sounds. It began with constant buzz from the millions of insects. It was succeeded by a strange sawing roar coming from the jaguar prop, with the surround sound being delivered by the Dolby stereo. This was followed by a loud scream originating from several colorful macaw flying.

Madan was playing the part of a hunter in a skit on the stage of his school. The audience was all-female. Before he realized, he was stark naked and impetuously making a futile attempt to cover his private parts. A few girls were giggling and few others were hooting, which sparked an unprecedented burst of catcalls towards Madan. To make matters worse, an anaconda prop sprung to life and coiled its muscular body around him to squeeze his pitiable life out of him.

Madan woke up with a loud shriek and his mother was startled by it. This was a recurring dream. This was fifth time in this year he had same dream of being naked in a forest. He didn't know if it meant anything and wasn't sure of how to cope with it. When his mother enquired him, he shook off any concerns and replied that probably had a nightmare.

DOCTOR VISIT

"Doctor, please castrate me. I deserve nothing less"

Madan was in the government hospital visiting a renowned female doctor. It was very old building which started as a humble army-dispensary during the British regime and was originally constructed with dressed-stone masonry. It consisted of majestic symmetrical three-storied buildings with a four-storied clock-tower in the center.

Doctor replied: "First tell me what is your problem? Did you injure your private part during masturbation?"

Madan: "With due respect Madam, you are not comprehending the gravity of the situation. I am not sure if you are the right person with whom I can share my concerns"

Doctor: "Never address me as Madam. It can be polite term or can also refer to a woman who is engaged in the business of procuring prostitutes. I don't want to be second guessing your intention"

Madan: "Sorry Madam. Err I meant sorry doctor. I don't know how to start"

Doctor: "It's ok. You can trust me that I will keep our conversation private. I have taken Hippocratic oath."

Madan: "I have committed a grave sin. No god will forgive

me no matter how much I repent"

Doctor: "Do we need to involve police? Did you commit any crime?"

Madan: "Yes. It is a crime which requires moral policing"

He started crying inconsolably and narrated the whole story.

"Last night, I had the weirdest nightmare. It was different from a recurring dream that riles me up. In that dream, I was in my birthday suit and sleeping next to my mother in our bedroom. My father suddenly barged into the room and he was out of his wits on seeing us. I was trying to explain him that I did no wrong but he started screaming and threw a few punches at me. I was so scared that I woke up shivering. To my horror, I also realized that I had ejaculated in my pants and because of that I am dying of embarrassment"

Doctor just sat there, flabbergasted. After pausing for a few seconds, she said: "You might not need an operation. I recommend you pay a visit to our psychologist"

Madan: "I heard psychologists in this city are expensive and charge exorbitant rates. I don't have so much money on me to pay their fees"

Doctor: "In that case, I will give you an off the record advice"

A fit middle-aged man in deep maroon-colored robe greeted Madan. They were meeting in the garden of a beautiful township nestled in a picturesque river valley. Beauty of the snow-capped mountains in the background was a sight to behold. Madan initially thought of wearing a woolen sweater, but since the wind was too strong and chilly, he put on a windcheater. He introduced himself to the man in front of him and curiously enquired how he didn't feel the cold as he was thinly dressed.

The man responded with a confident smile "You can call me Globe Baba"

Globe Baba was a renowned retired psychologist. He was well read man who was inspired mainly by the works of Sigmund Freud, Carl Jung and Osho. He was also a minimalist and wasn't enrolled into the rat race of the corporate world.

Globe Baba gave Madan a butt smack and guffawed "Haven't you seen sexy actresses showing their navel and busty cleavage in a similar backdrop? I bet you never complained then"

People say first impression is the last impression. Madan felt that he had wasted his time travelling to encounter a pervert. Madan's doctor had recommended that he meet Globe Baba, a spiritual soul and also arranged bus tickets to the picturesque hilly town. Hence, out of respect for his doctor, he decided to give Baba a second chance.

Globe Baba continued "So tell me young man. What brings you here to my gentle abode?"

To begin with, Madan spoke about his personal life and parents. Then he carefully narrated his recurring dream and later provided details about his dirty latest dream. As soon as he finished narrating the dream, he hung his head in shame.

"I hope you didn't discuss this wet dream with your friends. They would label you as a motherfucker for life" grinned Globe Baba, sporting his French beard.

Madan had it. He turned his back on the man and ambled towards the exit gate. Globe Baba ran up to him and gave him a warm hug.

Globe Baba: "Hey buddy! I noticed that you were very stressed since the moment you landed here. I cracked up a few lame jokes to break the ice. Madan, I will not ask you to trust me because trust cannot be gained by asking. If you want to continue the conversation, meet me here tomorrow at the break of dawn"

A congregation of nine women of varying ages and races wearing maroon robes were dancing wildly in a circle formation with arms raised to the sky. These women had different body shapes, hairstyles, and demeanors. At center of the circle, Madan spotted Globe Baba dancing like no one was watching. Globe Baba wasn't a bit surprised at seeing Madan the next morning. He excused himself from the dance by shouting "Stop the music" and joined Madan.

Globe Baba enquired "Are you still mad at me? Can we wait for a minute? I need to catch my breath—I can't dance as fast as young guys!"

Madan smiled and shook his head horizontally.

Globe Baba: "I will ask you some rapid-fire questions. You need be absolutely honest with me in your response"

Madan gave him a thumbs up and replied "Please shoot your questions at me"

Globe Baba started firing on all cylinders "Do you watch a lot of porn?"

"No. I have just watched one video in my entire life" Madan replied in a jiffy.

Globe Baba: "Which genre? Incest?"

Madan replied "I am not aware of any genres. It was a video of naked people becoming intimate"

Globe Baba: "How often do you masturbate?"

Madan: "I rarely do. I am a prisoner at home"

Globe Baba: "Do you love your mother?"

Madan snorted "I love her more than anything in this world. It is the purest form of love. Since my birth, she is painstakingly taking care of me all her by herself. And I had this dream..."

Globe Baba cut him short "Madan, you are completely normal. Your conscious and preconscious mind is clean. And you have no control over the unconscious"

"There is no foolproof method to interpret dreams. Your latest dream could be a classic case of Freud's positive Oedipus Complex theory. Your parent's broken marriage and your strict upbringing might have contributed to this dream.

To resolve this, you need to develop healthy sexual relationships with other women. If we don't resolve it soon, you might choose romantic partners that resemble your mother or become more possessive about your mother. I am pretty sure you don't want to end up as the real-life male lead who is sandwiched between Saas and Bahu" Babaji concluded.

"Yuck. I hate soap opera" Madan replied.

"You cannot image how many men in this world are torn between their mother and wife. If the mother wins, marriage might become a shambles and end up in divorce. If the wife wins, the couple might start a nuclear family and slowly break ties with husband's family" Globe Baba replied jovially.

"What if both of them win?" he innocently asked Globe Baba.

Globe Baba replied "The husband will lose his mind. A

man who had lobotomy surgery would fare far better than him"

"Babaji, and how will you explain my recurring dream of me being stark naked in a forest among wild animals and bevy of beauties?" a visibly impressed Madan questioned Baba.

"Being naked and seeing Anaconda / snake in your dream might represent your unconscious sexual desires. Jaguar might indicate that you will have a strong connection with a woman who menstruated during the Blood Moon. Macaw might indicate that you need to confront your problems in order to move forward in your life" replied Globe Baba earnestly.

An elated Madan returned to his home city satisfied by the answers provided by Globe Baba. His mother jumped in joy when she saw him and derided Globe Baba for keeping her away from her only son. He argued with his mother to give him more space in life.

Madan saved Globe Baba's contact on his phone and had him on speed dial so that he would never have trouble contacting him. In reality, he didn't need to worry as Globe Baba called him and woke him up to share his sexcapades every other day, before crowing of the rooster early in the morning.

Madan never had a goal until this point in his life. Now he had a goal – to pursue a girl and make her his girlfriend. He increased his interactions with the opposite sex in the hope of finding someone with whom he could have a healthy long-term relationship.

Madan thought to himself "I am a tall, fair and handsome guy. I often catch girls staring at me or bumping into me on purpose. Getting a girlfriend will be a piece of cake"

Alas! Madan quickly realized his folly.

After the first few dates, most of the girls either ignored or friend-zoned him. Luckily for him, after a few months, he found a girl who was really into him. They dated for a few months and on one Saturday night, the girl invited him home by saying that her parents weren't at home.

As they started getting cozy with their clothes on, Madan suffered from premature ejaculation. The girl started laughing at him and asked him to wash up. Once he returned, she asked him to suck her pussy. Madan leaned into her crotch area and put his tongue out. Before he could proceed any further, he was put off by her smell. The embarrassed girl asked him to go home.

Disappointed, he called up Babaji and asked for advice.

"First of all, let me clear your misconception regarding beautiful people. You might think that they have it easy in life. It is actually the other way round. While it is true that society rewards good-looking humans, it is also true that society has more expectations from them than an average Joe.

Imagine you are among the audience in Roman Colosseum or are watching a modern-day tennis match. Crowd and media favorite is usually the one who is more attractive physically. They will subconsciously cheer for that person and root for their victory. If the good-looking persons sweat it out and put in the hard yards, they might eventually hone their skills and win championships with the support of the crowd. If they are swayed by their short-lived popularity and play to the crowd, they might lose their focus on the game and are quickly forgotten.

Likewise, in relationships, beautiful people might struggle with Choice Paralysis as they are chased by too many suitors and more often than not end up choosing the wrong person. So, a beautiful person lacking values and goals might eventually end up losing or is exploited to the core. And surface beauty doesn't last forever, it can fade away anytime.

On the other hand, an average-looking / ugly person will try to compensate for their lack of physical beauty and usually has much more to offer in a relationship.

Irrespective of looks, eyes are the window to one's soul. Therefore, establishing a strong and honest eye to eye contact with the person you want to date is key first step to build trust" Globe Baba gave a lengthy response.

"Coming to your PME problem. You were brought up in a closed environment where masturbation is considered a taboo. You are so scared of being caught during masturbation, that you would want to end it as quickly as possible. In your particular case, your anxiety might be causing you to climax sooner than you would like.

People usually consider only the penis, vagina, anus, mouth and breasts as sexual organs. But my friend, they forget that it is the brain that controls everything and brain is without a doubt, the most important sex organ, at least in rational human beings. Masturbation, when not addictive, is healthy and relieves a person from stress. I would advise you to masturbate at least 1-2 hours before indulging in sex," said Globe Baba.

"Coming to the last point. You are an idiot who hurt that

poor girl's ego. Do you think your dick tastes like a delicacy? It is pivotal that people engaging in sex practice good hygiene. It is recommended to take bath and clean your private parts before the act. The problem with porn is that it sets wrong expectations with respect to human bodies and makes you idolize certain body types. Just remember that even a beautiful man or woman eats and shits like any other human being" Globe Baba censured Madan.

"Babaji, you have made me wiser with your advice. I have a complaint on society though. We have mock exams before the board, drills before playing an actual game etc. Similarly, why is that we don't have any practical coaching when it comes to matters of sex?" Madan asked sheepishly.

"Believe me, first-time sexual encounters are always weird. I vaguely remember the first time I got intimate with a woman. We actually didn't have sex. Both of us undressed quickly and she asked me to penetrate her using protection. At that time, I didn't know the importance of foreplay. She helped me wear a condom and spread her legs wide. I was shit scared and wasn't sure of how to kick it off. I nervously put my cock protected by rubber inside her and out of fear, took it out immediately. She was surprised and stared at my face. So, I repeated the same action around twenty times. Put it in and pull it out immediately"

"ROFL! and you don't classify that as love making?" Madan couldn't help but die laughing while responding.

Globe Baba replied in the negative.

"Jokes apart, what is your opinion on buying sex?" Madan asked.

"Did you know that Prostitution was practiced as a profession throughout cultures and is more than four thousand years old? You will be surprised to know that during those times, a significant chunk of prostitutes was male.

In the 20th century, there was rise of sexually transmitted diseases or STDs like gonorrhea, AIDS, chlamydia etc. and brothels were identified as hotspots for these diseases. There was also rise in exploitation of woman and sex trafficking, especially of children. Due to these reasons, several governments clamped down on legal prostitution.

There are a few developed countries where even now it is legal. However, almost every country has some or the other form of illegal prostitution and government / police tend to turn a blind eye as they are indirectly run by powerful people" added Globe Baba.

"So, what is the solution?" asked Madan impatiently.

"There are many pros and cons of prostitution. I don't have a readymade answer. Why don't you assess the current situation and solve this challenge?" Globe Baba challenged Madan.

"I understand the many bad aspects such as dehumanizing, exploitation, trafficking and loss of respect in society. Apart from the prospect of quick physical intimacy, I really don't see any advantages of this practice" Madan replied.

"Regular income, potential decrease in acts of sexual violence such as rapes, and low ratio of STDs in places where it is legalized, could be a few pros. In fact, a bunch of feminists that I know are in favor of decriminalization of prostitution" concluded Globe Baba.

Madan's goalpost had now shifted. He was now more concerned about solving problem of sexual training and awareness rather than finding a girlfriend. Madan got to know from his friends that the easiest way to get laid in his city was either by visiting a shady massage center or by swiping right on dating apps. He chose the former as he recollected seeing a massage center about 4 kms away from his home.

Madan reached his destination using a bike sharing app. It was an Asian massage center with windows made of tinted glass. Almost entire staff looked Chinese and wore skirts and low-cut tops. Upon Madan's enquiry regarding their native, the woman at the front desk replied that most of them were from the Seven Sister states or Northeast India. Due to lack of good opportunities back home, they had migrated to other parts of the country for work and were exploited as cheap labor. But they were as Indian as Madan was.

Madan apologized for his indiscretion and booked a full body massage for one hour. Receptionist asked Madan to go inside one of the rooms after removing his sandals. She allowed him inside only after she silently observed his mannerisms to confirm that he wasn't high on drugs or alcohol.

As soon as he entered the room, he noticed that there was

a legal notice on the wall prohibiting the customers and staff from indulging in any form of sexual activities. A middle-aged masseuse entered and asked him to undress quickly and lie on his stomach on the massage bed. Madan thanked his stars as this woman was as per his preference. He liked woman elder to him since his childhood as he believed they were physically and emotionally mature.

As she left the room for him to undress, he first carefully hid his wallet and expensive watch. Later, he quickly removes all his clothes except his underwear and was waiting on the bed with his head gazing at the floor. He felt a bit awkward as his underwear had two holes in it.

After two minutes, the lady was back and closed the room. She turned on light soothing music, turned off the smart bulb by prompting Alexa and lighted a couple of scented candles. She then applied some oil to Madan's body and started massaging with her masterful fingers. On the spur of the moment, she jumped onto the bed and placed her bent knees beside his torso. She started massage from top of his body, kneaded his head and neck area, spent a lot of time rubbing his back and then worked on his muscular legs. Madan could immediately feel decrease in stiffness and improved blood circulation. The lady asked him to turn over and lie on his back. This entire massage took about thirty-five minutes of time.

As he turned over, he got a bolt from the blue. Much to his disappointment, the masseuse was not the same lady who had earlier requested him to undress. She was much younger, way more leaner and wore a surgical mask to cover her face. She asked for his consent to massage his phallus and help him orgasm, that is give him a pleasurable hand job. When Madan nodded his head up and down, she removed his underwear in an instant and started stroking his cock.

After his last conversion with Babaji, Madan became adept at controlling his mind and thoughts. He kept thinking about various topics such as the last ball finish in the cricket match yesterday, his preparation for college etc. The young masseuse, who had initially started her strokes at a slow pace, picked up speed to make him cum quickly. After twenty minutes, she realized that Madan had only five minutes of time left and informed him that the clock is ticking.

"Is it possible to extend this session to another hour?" asked Madan brashly.

"No sir. I have another client to attend to after this session" she replied.

"What if I pay double rate for the next one hour? Can you cancel your existing appointment?" he asked.

"I am sorry sir. But it is not possible" she tiredly replied.

"Look lady. I didn't request for these extras. You offered it to me. But you didn't help me climax. Isn't it a case of bad customer service as you didn't deliver on your promise? Your parlor will not get five-star rating from me" Madan questioned her.

To his surprise, this question made her think and she went to front desk, had a conversation with receptionist and returned to the room.

"Ok sir. Let's continue for the next one hour. And you needn't pay a penny as I have settled it with the reception" she said.

And the "massage" restarted. The masseuse now made eye to eye contact while stroking him. She made sexy sounds during the act. Madan was no less than a mischievous brat. He was feeling the heat now and there was a buildup of tension but somehow, he managed to calm his mind again.

The masseuse was also up for the challenge. She was unleashing different arrows from her imaginary quiver and wished for one of those arrows to hit bullseye. She removed her crop top to reveal her boobs supported by a t-shirt bra, grabbed Madan's hands and placed them gently on her breasts. She wasn't going to remove her innerwear at any cost. Madan was quick to notice a crescent moon tattoo on her chest, situated right above her bosom.

Last but not least, she started talking to him openly without divulging any personal details. They chatted for about forty minutes, laughing and giggling all the while. Both of them looked at the stop clock again and it was seconds aways from hitting the two-hour mark.

Just when she was about to wave the white flag, Madan experienced a climax so intense that Shakespeare would have failed miserably to properly describe it in words. On second thought, maybe the feeling could be compared with a popular line from Chacha Chaudhary comics.

"When Sabu gets angry, a volcano erupts at some distant place in Jupiter"

Madan didn't message the massage girl for a month. Later, he paid a visit to the massage center to meet the same masseuse. The receptionist informed that the girl had quit her job and that she had no clue whatsoever of her whereabouts.

"Teacher. She is my teacher who introduced me to the joy of sex. I will never forget her in my life." Madan said to himself.

As for the girl, she forgot him immediately after that massage for he was just one of her innumerable clients.

Yue had reached the vast bustling city that was lively, with lot of people. She was on the lookout for her family lawyer. But how would she recognize him? She was a toddler when she escaped to the village and she wasn't sure if she would even be able to recollect the face of her real father. She was in a famous marketplace and was trying to buy some cheap food to silence her growling stomach.

An eight-year-old girl emerged out of the blue and stole money from Yue's pouch. She chased her down after running at full tilt for ten minutes and lifted her up in the air. She frisked the kid thoroughly several times but she couldn't find her pouch. Then she heard loud footsteps and noticed the shadow of two middle-aged men as it crept closer.

"Hand over the kid to us. She is urgently needed somewhere else" said the men.

Yue looked at the street urchin and realized that she didn't want to go with these men. The girl cried and said to Yue that she didn't want to leave her and satisfy the fetish of filthy rich old men anymore.

"Leave her alone. I will replace her and make money for you. However, if I ever get to know that you guys are harassing her, you will have to face my wrath" Yue yelled at the two rowdy men.

It took Yue a few days to realize that she had been scammed. The kid was a part of an elaborate scam to trap young ladies and force them into prostitution.

"No hard feelings Akka!" exclaimed the urchin.

Yue accepted the girl as the sibling she never had and named her Chloe. She asked Chloe to narrate her life story to understand how she ended up in this living hell.

Chloe casually replied "I am not really sure. My friends say that my parents were daily laborers and had five children. They sold me and my twin brother as babies to this gang in the city"

"Is your twin brother being forced to beg on the streets?" Yue enquired.

"No. He is also in my line, that is working as a child prostitute. As a matter of fact, he is in much more demand than me. Most of his customers are women and transsexual" Chloe guffawed.

When the two sisters were off their regular duty, they attended night college and after college hours, they donned their detective hats and searched every nook and corner of the city for clues relating to Yue's real family.

Yue was star walking on the main road when she spotted a huge hoarding advertising about the construction of new luxury gated communities. In the picture of one of their completed projects showcased as their credentials abroad, she observed a few tall buildings that felt very familiar.

Suddenly it struck her that these were the same building where she and her real dad used to walk every night. She immediately noted down the number mentioned under contact us and got hold of her lawyer.

Her family lawyer was dumbstruck. He thought Yue had also died on that fateful night and didn't expect Yue to return. Yue left her old life behind and started a new life. She focused on her higher studies and developed new hobbies.

After graduating from the distinguished Harvard University, she took over the reins of her father's empire and worked hard for many years to make it #1 in the world. She later spun off part of her business and started Venuxx, her brainchild.

She rescued Chloe from the slum and appointed her as her secretary after training her for a year. In fact, all the employees of Venuxx were actually women who were victims of sexual exploitation and abuse in the past, they were former porn stars, prostitutes or masseuses. She had digitally erased their abusive past and helped them to turn over a new leaf.

Madan had a creative bent of mind and didn't mind taking the less trodden road. After Madan graduated in Bachelor of Arts, he wanted to pursue entrepreneurship. He had to take care of his ailing mother. His mother hated the word "business" and shouted at Madan whenever he uttered it. He wasn't rich and didn't have any rich relatives or friends backing him. He belonged to the lower middle-class group, which is risk averse. As a general rule, it is people belonging to the high or the low-income group who are risk takers.

He received several love proposals during his college stint. He was a handsome young man with lot of energy. Though he interacted with some of these girls, he made it clear to them in the beginning that he was looking for a long-term relationship.

The lover archetype represents passion, intimacy, and emotional connection. This archetype is evident in a range of films like "Romeo Juliet, Devdas, Beauty and the Beast" and embodies a range of forms, from romantic to universal love. However, given his low economic status and popularity with girls, girls desired to only have him as a boyfriend and didn't consider him a husband material.

He briefly dated a girl named Anjali. Anjali came from a royal family infamous for their flashy display of wealth. She studied in Madan's rival college and was mesmerized by his looks and extraordinary performance on the stage during an inter-college dance competition. Their dating was mostly limited to talking for long hours on phone and liking each other's posts on social media. They broke up when she went to Australia to pursue MBA.

He frequently dreamt about Anjali and their relationship. After two years, Anjali returned to India and met Madan. Madan was still lost and jobless. He couldn't crack any job interviews as he lacked the motivation to work in a regular 9-to-5 job. But this never deterred him from pursuing his goal to improve health and sexual wellness. He knew he had to fight against all odds in order to reach his goal to provide value to society rather than earn big bucks for himself. Anjali realized that there was a huge market opportunity in this space and proposed that they start a company as co-founders to pursue their mutual goals. She won a gold medal in her MBA college and knew how to raise capital, run a start-up.

"I would like Globe Baba to be part of our team" Madan proposed to Anjali.

Anjali had met Babaji a few times and absolutely hated him. When she revealed to him that she recently post graduated in MBA from a top-notch college, Globe Baba joked that he was also MBA, that is "Married But Available".

"Globe Baba is an irresponsible man who claims to be spiritual but is always seen in the company of women. He is married and has three kids, who live separately from him. He didn't divorce his wife and is pursuing open relationships. He is a Bakchod who only gives Gyan and never takes action. He doesn't follow any particular religion and makes a mockery of the sanctity of marriage. His only strength is to form strong connections with people and learn their secrets" she thought to herself.

Anjali also knew that Madan revered Globe Baba and put him on pedestal. So, she finally relented and three of them founded a wellness company called Marxy. Madan took CEO role, Anjali was CTO / COO and Baba was CHRO / Marketing Head. Their product range included mental therapy, spa and massage services, fitness services, sex toys, condoms, and educational content on wellness in the form of social media reels and blogs.

Their USP or unique selling proposition, was to provide services of sex psychologists and trained practitioners, who were masters of sex and coordinated with clients to realize their sexual fantasies in a safe environment. Persons seeking these services were first evaluated by the certified psychologists, who would recommend if they really needed practical sessions. The client details, be it single or couple or a group, were kept confidential.

After an initial setback, mostly caused by religious organizations and red-tape, their business started to flourish. Globe Baba made promotional videos to spread awareness on sexual wellbeing as it is treated as a taboo subject across the world.

FAILED MARRIAGE

One day, Anjali professed her love for Madan and said that she wanted to marry him and become a partner in personal life as well. Madan also liked Anjali but he wasn't sure if his feeling towards her was of love or lust. He felt he was ready to abandon Brahmacharya and begin his Grihasta stage. So, he asked Globe Baba for advice.

"Never marry. You will suffer your entire life" Globe Baba shouted at a bewildered Madan.

"Then why the hell did you marry and have three children?" screamed Madan.

"I wasn't an enlightened soul back then. Take my advice: pack your stuff and run away as far as you can from this Anjali. You will thank me in the future" said Babaji.

"Shaadi ka laddoo - Jo khaye pachtaye jo na khaye pachtaye"

"Please clarify my original question" asked an irritable Madan.

"Lust is animalistic. The main difference between lust and love is that lust uses the other person to fulfill your desires whereas love is respecting each other and having no ego hiding behind in a relationship" said Globe baba quoting Osho.

Madan felt he had a mixed feeling, so he didn't pay heed to Globe baba's advice and married Anjali. He had a big fight with her family, especially her brother before marriage and eloped with her initially. Later Anjali's family spent millions on their marriage and Madan's frail mother, who was impressed by the pomp and show, gave the couple her blessings. Globe Baba didn't attend their marriage and gave some lame excuses.

Anjali didn't want to have children after marriage. She didn't want her body to go through the painful changes during pre and post pregnancy. Madan loved children and wanted to have at least two children, ideally one boy and one girl. He believed their children would replace them in the world when they died. To the contrary, Anjali felt parents producing children in an already over-populated Earth were essentially narcissists, who wanted to leave their imprint even after they left this physical world. So, they mutually agreed to adopt kids in future.

After marriage, Madan and Anjali stayed in a three-bedroom apartment like a nuclear family. They had sex on a regular basis and were extremely happy with each other. Alas! Fate had other plans. After a year into their marriage, Anjali realized that she was four months pregnant and visited the doctor to abort her baby. The doctor performed some scans which revealed a beautiful and healthy baby. Doctor said that there will be complications to perform abortion at this stage and that Anjali might die in the process.

Anjali and Madan decided to go ahead with the pregnancy. She requested the doctor for a normal delivery and made herself ready for it. In the tenth month of pregnancy, her water broke and Madan rushed her to the hospital. Doctor gave her an injection to go into labor and made an effort to deliver the baby normally for almost an entire day. Anjali was exhausted with all the pushing and was shouting in extreme pain. Due to some last-minute complications, doctors informed Madan that they would require his consent to perform Caesarean section.

Anjali's father, who was in the hospital, immediately consulted their Raj guru or royal priest. The royal priest performed several astrological calculations and advised them to go for a normal delivery despite extreme risk associated with it. As per priest, this would increase the chances of having a baby boy. Madan was having none of it. For him, the utmost priority was firstly the safety of his wife, followed by the safety of the baby.

Doctors went ahead with C-section and delivered a beautiful girl child to the couple. No words could describe the joy Madan felt when he held baby close to his chest for the first time. As he watched his defenseless baby crying out loud in his arms, he thought to himself "I might not be sure about my feelings in other scenarios. But what I am experiencing right now is definitely the purest form of love"

Madan had no clue about postpartum depression as such issues were never discussed in the open. The changes in

Anjali were so drastic that he wondered if this was the same woman he had married. They had a tough time changing diapers and managing their business, which led to constant fighting in their relationship along with a lot of bickering.

"Men are from Mars and Women are from Venus"

As their baby turned two, Anjali felt that both career and relationship were destroyed. She felt that he didn't love her anymore due to his ultimate love for daughter. They hardly indulged in any love making in last two years as their baby slept between them. They had hired a full-time nanny to take good care of their daughter. Eight hours of good sleep every day is recommended by doctors. They knew this fact pretty well as they were spearheading a global wellness company. However, they were sleeping for less than four hours a day on average.

Grandparents of their daughter were absolutely of no help to the couple. These were the same folks who pressurized them, since the day of their marriage, to give them a grandchild. Madan's mother could hardly take care of herself. Anjali's parents visited them once in two months for two to three days and played with their granddaughter for less than thirty minutes in a day. They were just happy to see the baby running, crying and doing potty in front of them. And then, they would give her a mobile phone to watch YouTube kids or play games.

Madan got really angry whenever they would hug his daughter in front of their relatives or friends. He wanted them to spend more quality time with her by taking her to park, talking to her to develop her language skills and engaging her in her favorite hobby, which was coloring. This led to a lot of friction between him and his in laws. Anjali felt that Madan had no respect for elders and was unhappy with the way he treated them.

"Weird sadistic pleasure parents get from seeing their children face the challenges of parenthood"

Filled with rage and in an attempt to make him suffer, Anjali filed a wrong case in the court against Madan, and divorced him and took the custody of their only child. She also sold her shares in their company and returned to her royal birthplace.

Madan somehow bailed himself out from jail and called Globe Baba at 2am in the night.

"What did I tell you? Didn't I warn you against marriage?" chuckled Globe Baba.

Madan was silent and didn't react.

"It might be a classic case of Electra Complex where the daughter and mother are competing with each other for possession of the father. And I always knew that Anjali was Machiavellian, possessing traits like indifference to morality, lack of empathy, and a strategic focus on self-interest" Babaji continued.

"And it might be your fault as well. You had a dream about Anjali and created a wife archetype in your mind. She will cook my favorite dishes daily, she will seduce me in a certain manner, she will not smoke etc. And when she didn't conform to that archetype, you were unhappy"

"I am extremely depressed and not sure if there is any meaning to my life now. How to handle this stress?" asked Madan.

"Your current needs are oscillating between love and self-actualization. You need to accept yourself with all your flaws. Your basic needs, which are physiological and safety, are already met" Baba alluded to Maslow's theory.

"And didn't you watch that movie, Arjun Reddy? In that movie, the protagonist's grandmother says "*Suffering is very personal, let him suffer*" after his girlfriend gets married to someone else. You need to suffer now. I don't know for how long you will suffer. The only way to come out of this is to find out your real love and also focus on your unfinished business, that is our company." said Globe Baba.

"Additionally, your libido or sexual motivation has decreased. So, I recommend that you exercise regularly, sleep well and follow a healthy diet. Get outside and date women until you find the one you really love" suggested Globe Baba.

Anjali's parents blamed Moon signs of the couple for their fate. Madan's Moon sign was Libra whereas Anjali's Moon sign was Aquarius. It is believed that Sun sign of a person reveals their outer self while the Moon sign reveals their real self.

THE CASUAL DATE

2030 has been an eventful year. Entire world is engulfed by chaos as situation between Yue and Madan reached stalemate. They are not seeing eye to eye, not communicating directly with each other and all the lunar projects were put on the backburner for a while. Madan felt that there was more to Yue than meets the eye and that she definitely had some skeletons in her closet. To break the current impasse, Yue asked Madan if he would like to go on a secret date with her. Madan agreed to the proposal without wasting time.

Chloe made travel arrangements for Madan and Globe Baba to Rio di Janeiro in Brazil. After landing at the airport, they spotted a driver holding a placard having Babaji's real name and boarded a sleek car. Both of them wore hats and covered their eyes with dark aviator sunglasses as they didn't want to be recognized in public. A journey in a normal car driving through such a thick rainforest would have taken them nine long hours. The car which they boarded was no ordinary car. It was an out-of-this-world flying car with features like vertical takeoff and landing, foldable wings and hybrid engines.

During their flight, they spotted macaws of various colors flying in the jungle. The flying car came to a halt in just three hours and landed on the banks of Amazon River.

They got down and boarded a private yacht to find Chloe waving at them playfully. A mellow yacht rock compassing elements of rock, jazz, and rhythm was playing in the background. Chloe shyly informed that Yue is in the main room waiting for Madan.

Madan left Babaji in Chloe's company and almost broke open the main door of the luxury yacht in his excitement. He could already feel the strong erection in his pants due to increased blood flow to the penis. He entered the room half-naked. What he saw next gave him the shock of his life.

A curvaceous Yue is standing on a king-sized bed, dressed only in her red bra and panty, while a giant green anaconda is coiled around her body. It is a scene straight out of Salma Hayek's movie "From Dusk till Dawn", except for the fact that the snake in the movie was a comparatively smaller Albino Burmese Python. The reptile's green coloration is patterned with black spots and stripes and its head is small compared to its body, with eyes and nostrils positioned on top. Anacondas first use their strong jaws to capture their prey and later use their muscular bodies to suffocate the prey before swallowing it whole. And it can eat a fully grown human.

Roar! Roar! Roar!

He quickly turned to his left to spot a jaguar with a collar tied to a window grill of the bedroom. Madan experienced an uncanny feeling of déjà vu or a sense of been there, done that. He realized that he is staring death in the face.

In the meantime, the snake slid down from Yue's body and used serpentine and sidewinding locomotion to slither forward towards Madan. Yue expected him to make a run for it. To Yue's and Anaconda's surprise, Madan started laughing out maniacally.

"Vinash kale viprit buddhi"

Madan had spotted a tattoo on Yue's chest. He could never forget that tattoo nor his teacher. It was tattoo of the Crescent Moon. It dawned on him that Yue was the masseuse he met many years ago and was his true love. Surprisingly, the snake didn't attack Madan, jumped in to the river and disappeared into the thick jungle.

If you really want something, the whole universe conspires in helping you achieve it. No Man or Woman, however, powerful they might be, can stop things destined to happen.

Yue feigned ignorance, remarked that he was lucky to survive and asked him to leave. Madan stepped outside and started looking for Globe Baba to share this news and express his happiness. Babaji was nowhere to be found. He heard loud banging noises coming from toilet and climbed down the stairs in the Yacht. Chloe and Baba were fucking each other despite an age gap of thirty years between the two of them. And it was staggering that the sex was consensual.

Madan lifted a bottle of red wine lying near the mini bar and finished it without putting the bottle down. Bottoms up! Then he started crying and threw empty beer cans at Babaji.

"After all these years, I finally found the woman I truly love and she doesn't love me back. At the other end of spectrum, we have Globe Baba. Every other woman is fucking this old man". Madan cried his heart out.

Chloe giggled, put on some clothes and covered Babaji with a towel. She then narrated Yue's entire backstory to Madan and explained her connection with snakes. Yue found a python's egg during the Blood Moon when she was a kid. She raised the python secretly in the forest behind her house and managed to tame it. This was the same python that had killed Eramma.

She also confirmed that Yue worked as a masseuse for many years in the same city where Madan lived. Customers who visited the massage center were usually filled with lust and treated staff like mere objects. They would visit, fuck and forget. Some clients hit them or forced them to do disgusting and perverted acts. Yue treated all her customers the same except for one. She fell in love with his character, charm, and grace. He was the only guy at the parlor to talk to her with an open heart and empathy. And she secretly worshipped him all these years. The man was none other than Madan.

Madan was jumping and dancing in joy. Tears tricked down Globe Baba's face. Madan had never seen him crying till date.

"Billionaire businessman missing for one week dies at age 50"

Newspapers and media went crazy. It was Breaking News on all channels. Videos went viral within microseconds on social media. The mystery deepened as the body of the missing eccentric billionaire was found floating in the Amazon River. The body was badly decomposed and post mortem report of his remains confirmed the date of his death as one week ago and reason of his death as drowning and Ischemia, restriction in blood supply to organs.

Madan and Globe Baba stared at each other's face in agony when then read this news on their phones and started sweating. They had just returned from their awesome adventure in the Brazilian rainforest. They knew exactly how he might have died. Madan vaguely recollected that Chloe had planned an appointment between Yue and businessman a few days ago. But what could be Yue's motivation to get him killed? If she wasn't interested in him, she could have rejected his moves instead of egging him on.

A few moments ago, Madan was planning to propose to Yue. He made plans to book their travel to the Moon on his rocket and propose to her among the stars. But things are so topsy-turvy now.

"Is Yue really a cold-blooded murderer? Death of her adopted mother, Eramma, is probably justified. How many other men and women have been suffocated by such giant snakes and perished? Can these deaths be somehow connected to assassination of Yue's father? Is she out to take revenge?" his mind was racing faster than a F1 racing car.

Madan decided to secretly investigate this death. He received an invitation to an exclusive dinner party in Venice thrown by some members of the Luna Accords. Party would be preceded by a game of golf. Madan normally didn't attend such parties as they sucked. He felt that guests were a bunch of douchebags being phony to each other. He was pretty sure that Yue would have also received this invite. That would be his best chance to interrogate her indirectly and get more leads on the case.

Golf is a slow-paced and less exciting game for a sigma male in his mid-thirties. It is a game created for the rich and is filthy expensive. It lacks action like football or tennis, both of which involve a lot of running. Madan yawned as he watched a group of elderly men swinging their clubs in Venice.

The old men stopped their game abruptly and jogged towards a lady dressed in sexy leotard. Madan could recognize her from a distance. Of course, It was Yue. As Yue was selecting golf club for her next swing, the horny old men started touching her inappropriately while engaging her in boring conversation. They were debating on the numbers of holes in a woman versus number of holes in the 7000 yards golf course.

"3 vs 10, 10 vs 10, 2 vs 18"

These wealthy men were old enough to be their grandfathers. Even if they took the most potent Viagra in market, they might not get an erection. Then why is that majority of the rich old men and women feel the urge to abuse and exploit the weak.

"Human Sexuality begins in the infant stage and continues to grow over time until death. Your school teacher, your boss, your relatives…everyone has a sexual energy. And this is what happens if they don't manage their libido properly" answered Globe Baba by second-guessing Madan's thoughts.

There is a complicated relationship between Power and Sexuality. The Strong oppress the Weak. Abuse of power is not restricted to any sex or religion or caste or profession or income or political group or company or country.

Muslim rulers maintained a harem, where he, his wife, his daughters lived along with concubines and were guarded by castrated men. Devadasis, touted as daughters of God, were offered by parents to temples, and were exploited by Hindu priests. A few Catholic popes have been found guilty of sexual abusing young boys and nuns. Gautam Buddha is believed to have led a colorful life before he attained enlightenment.

In modern day, we hear news of CEOs being fired as they sexually harassed their subordinate. At the same time, we also hear news of poor people raping and killing innocent souls.

The rich always felt powerful. And with great power, comes great responsibility. At least that's what spiderman said. Now might be a good time for some of these C-suite folks, who wear suits daily, to revisit their childhood and revise their superhero comics. The abbreviation CEO should also stand for Chief Ethical Officer apart from Chief Executive Officer.

One can't imagine the audacity of many of these sexual abusers. They occupy a seat in the POCSO (Protection of Children from Sexual Offences) or POSH (Prevention of Sexual Harassment Committee) teams or talk about reforms against sexual exploitation. In most of the cases, their "success" shields them from being convicted in this maya called life. The sheer hypocrisy of such a situation is enough to make anyone's blood boil.

Sex is a gift of life that should be relished. It should never be a form of oppression. Fantasies such as BDSM exist, but bottom line is that there needs to be CONSENT of every creature indulging in the act with a human.

The way Yue played golf changed Madan's opinion about the sport. He understood that the game was challenging and demanded skill. Yue received a phone call and she instantly left the golf course. Madan tailed her to keep her under his surveillance.

Yue was talking to an executive from her former real estate company. He informed her that there have been a series of mysterious deaths since her father died. They used big data analytics to find out the common link between all the deaths.

"All the people who died bought a piece of land on the Moon. This list includes your deceased father, politicians, businessmen, actors, sportsmen, musicians etc. Unknown to us, some illegal companies have been secretly drilling small portions of the Moon using robots since many years" the executive revealed to Yue.

"So that's how my favorite Rabbit on the Moon vanished" she thought to herself.

There are no laws regarding ownership of celestial bodies. A few gullible people have been cheated by rouge agents to spend their lifetime worth savings on investment in land on the Moon. If a space agency, supported by our tax money, mines the Moon or an asteroid for valuable minerals, it would never share the profits with rest of the world. Billionaires will turn into Zillionaires and will potentially enslave the world with the power of money.

"Do we know which organization or country is behind all these killings"? she questioned him.

"That is still a mystery and even our most advanced technologies are not able to figure that out" he replied.

Madan heard the entire intimate discussion with his own ears and he still could not make up his mind if Yue is on a revenge spree. He realized that both Yue and he were late for the stupid party. He was startled by a frantic phone call from Globe Baba.

"While we were partying near the canals under the full Moon, high tides caused sudden flooding of the venue and lives of many of the prominent guests such as old men who played golf today, couldn't be saved. I clung onto a big door and somehow managed to save myself" informed a fatigued Globe Baba.

The impact of the high tide and subsequent flooding was particularly devastating to low-lying coastal areas around the world. Many people lost their lives and families. Scientists are blaming a wobble in the orbit of the Moon for the high-tide floods. As per them, this phenomenon occurs every 18.6 years. A few cities across the world have submerged entirely like the fictional Atlantis city or ancient city of Dwarka.

Yue had no patience left. She realized that somehow everything is connected to the Moon. Chloe had leaked Madan's romantic date plan on the Moon to Yue. Yue asked Madan to take her to the Moon in his space rocket as soon as possible.

"But…Today is not 14th February…Valentines Day" replied Madan.

"Are you out of your mind? People are dying everywhere. We can't wait any longer. We have the means and all the right reasons to investigate and get to the bottom of this mystery before more people die" she replied in anger.

Yue and Madan boarded the most powerful rocket and started their journey to the Moon. This manned mission was fraught with extreme danger as no man or woman dared to do this in the last fifty years. Madan was happy that both of them were finally all alone and that Yue clutched onto his hand tightly during blast off.

"Why did you kill that businessman and throw his body into the river?" Madan asked her boldly to kill time.

"Why would I kill him? While it is true that we planned to have a meeting to discuss a lunar project, he never met me on the day of our appointment. My theatrics on the luxury yacht are just a tactic to scare cowardly men to stop hitting on me. I never intend to kill anybody" Yue replied.

"What about Eramma's death then? I am sure you will admit to your role in her death" asked Madan.

"Her death was sheer coincidence. My python was hungry for months and was silently sizing up Eramma's proportions whenever entered the forest to collect wood. And that night, it randomly attacked and killed her. It is after all a wild animal and not a fancy pet" she revealed.

Both of them took a nap for two hours. After they woke up, they could see a pale blue dot in the darkness of space. They wondered about the origin of universe and discussed if there could be life elsewhere on any one of the planets /moons in 100 billion galaxies.

It took them a total six hours to reach the Moon and to land safely on the dark side of the Moon. They put on their space suits and as they were setting their feet on the Moon, they had a strange feeling that they were being watched. Apollo astronauts who landed on the Moon in 1969 also hinted at a similar eerie experience.

After taking a few leaps on the Moon, they spotted a device looking like an audio machine and approached it. They spotted two buttons on it and Yue quickly touched one of the buttons randomly.

Yue talked something in English and waited for something to happen. All of sudden, they heard an audio message playing.

"Humans on Earth. Please remember that you are not alone. You are but a miniscule speck in vastness of the universe. We have been monitoring you since ancient times and controlling your nuclear might and space expeditions. UFOs that some of you spotted and reported are actually our flying machines. Some of our descendants are still hiding on Earth.

You will be surprised to know that we control not only your water bodies but also your sleep and dreams. Your sleep hormone, Melatonin, was introduced into humans by us. Your dreams are not random, they are some incidents taking place somewhere else in a multiverse. What you perceive as your reality might be a dream for someone else in another universe. We are all connected as we are all made up of the same space matter.

Didn't you ever wonder why you experienced paranoia or depression due to sleep deprivation? Or why your immunity is reduced if you suffer from insomnia? Or why your eyes, which are gateway to your souls, darken due to lack of sleep?

We can trick your mind and make it believe that creatures in your nightmares like ghosts, vampires, werewolves and other evil exist. Only a few extraordinary humans who were able to control their minds were able to understand these facts.

You all are children of Mother Earth. The Moon was formed after our planet from another universe collided with Earth millions of years ago. We have no objection to cooperate if you come in peace. However, if you lust for our resources disregarding sanctity of matter on the Moon, you will have to face dire consequences"

Yue felt that this message was a joke and was created by some company using generative AI on Earth.

"If you are really not from Earth, then show yourself to us" she shouted on the device.

Immediately, the surface of the Moon started shaking due to a seismic tremor. Madan and Yue started running towards their rocket. Unknowingly, Yue stepped on a small crater, which opened up to show a big hole. They felt they could see the shadows of some strange creatures emerging from the hole.

They somehow escaped and returned back to Earth safely. The message from the universe was loud and clear.

"Fix your home first before you look out for another"

Watch out for my next book

Tryst with gluttony